MY BROTHER BERNADETTE

This edition first published in Great Britain 2001
by Egmont Books Limited
239 Kensington High Street
London W8 6SA

Text copyright © Jacqueline Wilson 1995
Illustrations copyright © David Roberts 2001

The author and illustrator have asserted their moral rights

ISBN 978 0 7497 4223 2

7 9 10 8

A CIP catalogue record for this title is available from the British Library

Printed in Singapore

MY BROTHER BERNADETTE

JACQUELINE WILSON

Illustrated by David Roberts

YELLOW Bananas

For John Hastings
How Bernard would like
to be in his class!
J.W.

For Paul Harniess
D.R.

Chapter 1

'I DON'T THINK I want to go to this summer project,' said Bernard at breakfast.

'Yes, you do,' said Dad firmly.

'Sara will look after you,' said Mum, putting her arm round Bernard and giving him a cuddle.

I'm Sara. I'm Bernard's big sister and I always get lumbered with looking after my little brother.

'The summer project will be great,' I said, licking honey off my toast. 'There's going to be football and computer games and drama and heaps of other stuff. You'll love it, Bernard,' I said, though I wasn't absolutely sure he would. My little brother Bernard is a bit weird.

'Eat your toast properly, Sara,' said Mum. 'And you eat up too, Bernard.'

Bernard bent over his plate, cutting his toast into tiny little squares, the way he likes it.

'Stop being so finicky, Bernard,' said Dad. 'Come on, if you're quick I'll walk you both over to the summer project on the way to work.'

They've set up the summer project in the school next to our estate. It's being held for a whole month this summer. All the kids on the estate are going. We're all a bit older than Bernard, but Bernard's bright, so they said he could go too.

'I don't want to go,' Bernard said again.

But Dad made him.

'It'll do you good to have a bit of fun,' he said.

A helper took hold of Bernard's hand.

'Cheer up, pal,' he said. 'What would you like to do this morning, eh?'

'I want to play football,' I said. 'Come and watch me, Bernard.'

The helper decided that Bernard had to choose an activity for himself. Bernard didn't want to play football or baseball or judo or trampolining.

'What about model car making?' said
the helper.

'All right,' said Bernard.

My brother Bernard's good at making models.
He's got little Plasticine animals trekking up and
down our bedroom windowsill and his model
aeroplanes zoom above our heads.

Bernard quite fancied the idea of making model cars. He thought they'd be little cars, but these model cars were big ones. Another helper was showing children how to make cars with wheels and planks of wood. These cars were big enough to ride on.

Bernard made his own model car with a bit of help, no problem. He even perched up on it and went for a very short, slow ride.

But there were a lot of big boys making model cars too. Big Dan was the biggest boy of all. Big Dan is famous on our estate. We all try to keep out of his way.

Big Dan made a big car. He drove it like a dodgem but he didn't dodge. He drove bang into my brother.

Bernard fell off his car. He banged his head and hurt his hands. He tried not to cry but he didn't quite manage it.

The helper picked him up and comforted him. He told Big Dan that he was big enough to know better.

'Poor little Bernard,' said the helper.

Big Dan pulled a terrible face at Bernard.

'Poor little Bernard!' he said, mimicking. 'You stupid sissy little baby. You're like a girl with all that long hair. Bernadette, more like. Yeah. That's your new name. Bernadette.'

Chapter 2

MY BROTHER BERNADETTE didn't like his new name at all.

'My name's Bernard,' he said. 'Not Bernadette.'

Big Dan kept on calling him Bernadette. So the other boys did too. Then the girls joined in. By going home time everyone at the summer project was calling him Bernadette.

Poor Bernard went very pink in the face.

'His name's *Bernard*,' I said. 'You lot shut up, do you hear me? Stop calling him silly names.'

I can't stand it when anyone teases my brother Bernard. *I* tease him sometimes, but that's different. I'm his big sister.

I'm big but I'm not that big. I'm not anywhere near as big as Big Dan. I couldn't *make* him shut up.

'Bernadette,' yelled Big Dan, and ruffled Bernard's hair and poked him in the chest. He poked him lots of times, until Bernard fell over. Again.

I pulled him up quickly, but the helper had seen me and asked if Bernard was all right.

I fidgeted. I know you're are supposed to tell a helper if you are in trouble. I also knew if we told, Big Dan and his mates might get even worse.

'I'm fine, thank you,' said Bernard, in a very small voice.

We could fool the helper, but we couldn't fool Mum.

'Did you fall over, Bernard?' she asked. 'Look at your knees, love! And your hands! And is that a big bump on your head?'

'Yes!' said Bernard.

He was still having a cuddle with Mum when Dad got in.

'Hey there, kids! Did you have fun at the summer project?' he asked eagerly.

'*I* didn't have very much fun, Dad,' said Bernard.

'Big Dan kept pushing him over!' Mum said. 'In fact, they all kept picking on him and calling him names. He's not going back.'

'I don't want to go back,' said Bernard.

But he had to go back. Dad said so.

'He's got to learn to cope with a bit of rough stuff. I think you molly-coddle him far too much. He's got to toughen up a bit,' said Dad.

Mum and Dad had a big argument. Bernard and I crept to our bedroom. Bernie made a Plasticine Big Dan. We dive-bombed him with the aeroplanes. It was fun. Bernard cheered up a bit.

He wasn't so cheerful in the morning.

'Dad says you ought to give the summer project one more try, Bernard,' said Mum.

'I don't want to,' said Bernard.

'You've got to learn how to get on with the other boys, Bernard,' said Dad.

'They don't want to be friends, Dad,' said Bernard.

'This is awful! They're all so much bigger than him!' said Mum. 'Look, he's not going. I'll take the day off work to look after him.'

'You can't keep taking days off work. You'll lose your job,' said Dad.

'Well, maybe Gran could look after him,' said Mum.

'No, it's staying round at his Gran's so often that's turned him into a softie,' said Dad.

Bernard bent his head over his plate and cut up his toast into teeny tiny squares.

'Don't worry, Bernard,' I hissed. 'I'll look after you.'

But I wasn't sure that I could.

Chapter 3

THE CHILDREN STARTED yelling the minute they spotted Bernard.

'Bernadette! Here comes Bernadette!'

Big Dan came swaggering up.

'Ooh look, it's little Bernadette!' he said.

I tried to hurry Bernard away.

Big Dan came after us.

'Here, Bernadette, I'm talking to you.'

'Well, we don't want to talk to *you*, do we, Bernard?' I said.

Another helper came up to us.

'Everything all right, kids?' she said. 'Right, what activity is everyone going to do today?'

'We're going to race our cars,' said Big Dan. 'Wow, pow, wheeee! Come on, guys. Come on, Bernadette.'

Bernard wisely stood his ground.

'What would you like to do today?' said the helper, taking his hand.

'I don't know what I want to do,' said Bernard. 'I know what I *don't* want to do and that's model car making.'

'I think you might well be just the chap for computer games,' said the helper.

But the computer games were so popular that all the places were already taken.

The helper and Bernard mooched around
looking for something he wanted to do. I went
with him. All my pals called to me to come and
join their football team again, but I'd made a
promise and I was going to keep it.

'I can't,' I said. 'I've got to look after my
brother.'

'How about drama?' said the helper, as we
walked past the classroom windows towards
the main hall.

'Oh yeah, let's do drama, Bernard,' I said. 'I love acting.'

'I don't think I do,' said Bernard. Suddenly he stopped and peered into a classroom window. 'What are they doing in there?' he asked.

'That's clothes design,' said the helper. 'There's all sorts of jumble sale clothes and ribbon and flowers and stuff, and everyone can design their own creations.'

'*Sewing!*' I said. 'Boring. Come on, Bernard, let's do drama.'

'I want to do sewing,' he said.

'Great,' said the helper.

'You can't do sewing, Bernard!' I said. 'That's for girls.'

'It's for everyone, Sara,' said the helper.

Whatever she said, *I* knew that if Bernard did clothes design every single kid on our estate would call him Bernadette for ever.

Chapter 4

YOU CAN'T ARGUE with my brother Bernard.
He never ever gives in.

Bernard wanted to do sewing. So that's what
he did.

And I did it too. I thought I'd better keep an
eye on him. I felt bad that I'd rushed off to play
football yesterday. There was *one* good thing
about it. Big Dan wasn't going to want to sew.

At least the helper doing clothes design
looked interesting. She had long red hair and a
red dress and an embroidered waistcoat. She
looked up and smiled at us as Bernard and I

went into the classroom. All the other kids
looked up too.

'Hey – it's Bernadette,' said one girl, and she
and her pal started spluttering as they tried to
stop laughing.

'Hello, Bernadette,' said the helper, nodding
at me.

I shook my head.

'I'm not Bernadette. I'm Sara,' I said fiercely.
'And this is my brother Bernard. There are no
Bernadettes here. And anyone who says there
are is going to get beaten up.'

I glared at the girls. They stopped spluttering
sharpish.

'Right. Got it,' said the helper. 'Come and sort
through the jumble clothes, Sara and Bernard.
See if there's anything you fancy. And then
there's a bead box here, and some really wacky
artificial flowers and there are ribbons and
rickrack braid here.'

'Wow,' said Bernard, eyes shining. He started
ferreting through the clothes, picking out an old
Japanese kimono and stroking its silkiness.

28

'Don't you dare dress up in that, Bernard,' I hissed.

All he needed now was to start prancing around in a frock!

Bernard sniffed at the idea, but he kept the kimono tucked under one arm.

'Are we allowed to cut some of this stuff, Miss?' he asked.

'Sure,' said the helper. 'That's the whole idea. You two find what you want to work on and then I'll help you pin it and show you how to sew.'

'I can sew already,' said Bernard proudly.

'No you can't,' I said. '*I* can't sew. So you can't either.'

'I can too. Gran showed me how. I sewed on buttons. And I can do over-and-over sewing too. And I expect I can do this sort of picture sewing as well,' said Bernard, fingering the embroidered dragon on the kimono.

My brother Bernard is a little boy but he has big ideas.

He wasn't that good at sewing. The helper
suggested we practise a bit on a square of felt.
Bernard's stitches were rather big and wobbly.
I suppose they were sewing, of a sort.

Better than my stitches actually.

'You're doing well, both of you,' said the
helper. 'So you can get started on your actual
design now.'

'Bernadette's going to design a dress,'
whispered one of the girls.

Bernard's arm went out as he pulled on his
long thread. Accidentally on purpose his elbow
dug into the girl's side. Bernard's elbows are
extremely sharp. Maybe, just maybe, he's
learning to look after himself at last.

Chapter 5

I CERTAINLY DIDN'T fancy the idea of making myself a frock. I found some old jeans in the jumble pile and thought I'd cut off the legs and turn them into shorts.

'That's a good idea, Sara,' said the helper.

I went a bit mad with the scissors though. I went chop, chop, chop a little too enthusiastically. And once one leg had gone I had to cut the other one to match.

My shorts were certainly short. They were the shortest shorts ever. So short that they showed my knickers.

'Maybe you could have a little border on them?' said the helper, tactfully.

She got this blue and white check material and helped me cut it out. Well, she did all the cutting, actually. Then she pinned it to the edges of my shorts and sewed a tiny bit to show me how to do it. Then it was my turn. I had to sew. And sew and sew. It was so *BORING*.

Bernard didn't seem the slightest bit bored. He'd found a baseball jacket in the jumble pile. It was too big for him but it looked quite cute on him all the same. It made him look a lot tougher.

'I like it,' said Bernard.

'We can shorten the sleeves a bit,' said the helper.

'I like them long,' said Bernard. 'What I want to do is put a picture on the back. A sewing one, like the pictures on the Japanese dressing-gown thingy.'

'Hmmm,' said the helper doubtfully, but she did try to help. She got some felt and showed Bernard how to embroider a little flower.

'This is a lazy daisy stitch,' she said.

'Lazy daisy,' Bernard repeated solemnly, and had a go. And another and another.

He stitched for an entire hour, until the felt was all grey and sticky, and covered with chains of wobbly lazy daisies.

'Very good, Bernard,' said the helper. 'You can sew some daisies on your jacket now.'

'I don't want daisies,' said Bernard, 'I want a dragon.'

'Ah. Well . . . it would take months of practice before you're at the dragon stage,' said the helper. 'Unless . . . I know!'

She spread the kimono out and carefully cut right round the embroidered dragon.

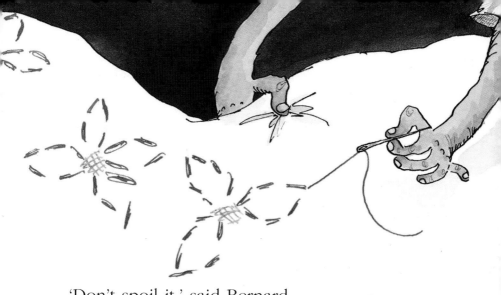

'Don't spoil it,' said Bernard.

He didn't need to worry. She was leaving quite a bit of edge around the stitches.

'Now!' she said, pinning the dragon into place on the back of the jacket. 'All we have to do is stitch round the edge – and you've got a dragon on your jacket.'

'Great!' said Bernard. It was the sort of over-and-over sewing that Gran had taught him. He was getting better and better at it.

By the time we broke up for lunch he'd finished it. He had an embroidered golden dragon breathing scarlet threads of fire on the back of his jacket. It looked fantastic.

'Look at Bernadette's jacket! I wish I had one like that.'

'Hey, show us how you made it, Bernadette. Can we have a bit of embroidery from the kimono?'

'Will you sew that little Japanese lady on the front of my frock, Bernadette, please?'

The girls gathered round him.

'Maybe,' said Bernard loftily. 'What's my name?'

They soon realised what he meant.

'Bernard. Your name's Bernard. Will you sew my bit first, eh, Bernard?'

Bernard helped them with their sewing all afternoon and I was able to slope off and play football.

I did *not* play football in my new shorts. It would have been my turn to be teased if I had.

Chapter 6

I PLAYED FOOTBALL most afternoons at the summer project, but I went to drama in the mornings. We had a really cracking time, even when Big Dan and some of his gang decided to give it a go too. We had this helper, Len, who was much much bigger than Big Dan.

'You ought to give drama a try, Bernard,' I said. 'It's ever such fun, honest. We're going to do a play for the end of the project. Why don't you be in it too?'

'No thanks,' said Bernard.

'It'll be okay about Big Dan, honest. He's as good as gold with Len. He wouldn't dare call you Bernadette.'

'No one calls me Bernadette now,' said Bernard.

He was right. All the girls in design called him Bernard. Some of the boys called him Bernie or Little Bern. He was getting quite popular. Everyone kept bringing him their old jackets so he could sew something startling on the back. He'd used up every bit of the embroidery on the Japanese kimono, but his helper found some tapestry and an old Swiss blouse and some velvet curtains with a moon

and star pattern. Bernard cut them out carefully
and sorted them out and sewed bits here and
bits there and it all worked a treat.

He even made his helper
a starry waistcoat.

My brother Bernard had
become a little star himself.

'I can't do drama, Sara,' he
said, humming happily. 'I'm
too busy doing design.'

Our drama group asked
Bernard's design lot if they
could help us with our
costumes for our end-of-
project play. We didn't
need anything really fancy,

as the play was about these two tough gangs and how a boy from one gang fell in love with a girl from the other gang.

I was the girl. The main part. I was dead chuffed about that.

Big Dan was one of the rival gang. I was terrified I'd have to fall in love with *him*. Yuck!

Len chose this other boy instead, and said Big Dan had better be the leader of the gang instead. He liked that idea.

Our gang was called the Blue Denims, so we didn't need new costumes, we could just wear our own jeans. Big Dan's gang was called the Black Leathers.

Big Dan came barging into Bernard's classroom.

'Hey, Bernadette, you're supposed to be good at this costume lark. Typical, you little sissy! Anyway, me and my gang need black leather costumes, right?'

'No, it's not all right' said the design helper.
'You can't come barging in here calling people
names and giving orders.'

'It's okay,' said Bernard. 'I'll make you and
your gang some black leather costumes, Big
Dan.'

'Will you? Yeah, well, good. Thanks . . .
Bernadette.'

My brother Bernard simply nodded and
smiled.

I thought it was a bit strange.

'I don't know about these black leather
costumes,' said the helper. 'No one gives
leather to jumbles because it's so expensive.
We haven't got any leather and I can't think
of anything that looks like leather.'

'I can,' said Bernard. 'Black plastic rubbish bags. Big strong ones so they don't split.'

Everyone thought it was a brilliant idea. It was tricky cutting out pretend black leather jeans and pretend black leather jackets. They glued the seams as there wasn't much time for stitching.

'We could sew some stuff on the back of the jackets, couldn't we?' said Bernard. 'We could use silver thread so it looked like studs.'

It took so long there wasn't time for a dress rehearsal.

'They'll be ready for the performance though, don't worry,' said Bernard.

He took the biggest black plastic jacket home with him and spent hours and hours stitching in secret.

'What are you up to, Bernard?' I asked. 'Why are you taking so much trouble for Big Dan?'

'You'll see,' said my brother and he smiled.

I did see, the next day, when we came to do the play. We all saw.

Bernard handed Big Dan his new black plastic jacket. It was a work of art. Bernard had embroidered hundreds of pink lazy daisies all over it. He'd sewn a message on the back too. *Daisy Dan.*

'I'm not wearing that poncy rubbish,' said
Big Dan.

He tried to grab one of the other jackets, but
they were all too small for him.

'You'll wear your own jacket,' said Len,
forcibly helping him into it, and he pushed Big
Dan on stage.

We all fell about when we saw him looking
so stupid in his daisy jacket.

'Look what Bernard's sewn for Big Dan!'

'Oh Bernie, you are a scream!'

'Hey, Daisy Dan, I like your flowers!'

No one calls my brother Bernadette any
more, but we've all got a brilliant new
nickname for Big Dan!

Yellow Bananas

Yellow Bananas are bright, funny, brilliantly imaginative
stories written by some of today's top writers. All the
books are beautifully illustrated in full colour.

*So if you've enjoyed this story,
why not pick another from the bunch?*

Author	Title	ISBN
KEVIN CROSSLEY-HOLLAND	Storm	07497 4698 X
MALACHY DOYLE	Long Grey Norris	14052 0594 6
ANNE FINE	Design a Pram	14052 0113 7
ANNE FINE	Countdown	07497 4672 6
ANNE FINE	Scaredy Cat	14052 0251 3
JAMILA GAVIN	Deadly Friend	14052 0113 9
JAMILA GAVIN	Fine Feathered Friend	07497 4224 0
ROSE IMPEY	Who's a Clever Girl, Then?	14052 0480 X
PENELOPE LIVELY	Dragon Trouble	14052 0132 0
MICHAEL MORPURGO	Conker	14052 0257 2
MICHAEL MORPURGO	Colly's Barn	14052 0255 6
MICHAEL MORPURGO	Snakes and Ladders	14052 0134 7
JACQUELINE WILSON	My Brother Bernadette	07497 4223 2